Two Critical Issues – One Innovative Solution

Dear Parent, Grandparent, Educator, and Concerned Adult:

It may surprise you to discover that although I'm an author, I don't like to read. **I love to read!** Since the start of the new millennium, The **It's A Habit!** Company, Inc. has had the privilege of demonstrating its passion for reading and sharing the **saving is a habit** message with thousands of elementary school students and educators.

We are pleased to report that both students and educators have enthusiastically embraced our message. Their letters express their excitement in implementing the lessons they've learned from the readings and presentations such as – **"I Love to Read"** ©, **"From Brain to Book"** ©, **"What's Bigger than Big?"** © and **"What a Dime in Time Will Do!"** ©. Our goal is to take these messages nationwide through our book series **The Adventures of Sammy the Saver**.

As most of us already know, literacy and financial illiteracy among children are serious national issues crossing all ethnic, social and economic boundaries. The consequences of not reading or saving are severe. The stakes are high. William Damon addresses this issue in his book *Greater Expectations - Overcoming the Culture of Indulgence in America's Homes and Schools:* "The stakes in the battle are the lives and future hopes of our young."

Learning to read and save are perhaps two of the most crucial lessons that we can teach our children. I'm glad my parents, grandparents and teachers taught me. As loved ones who deeply care about the future of our children and who are responsible for the teaching of appropriate reading, spending and saving behaviors, we have a choice. We can instill attitudes and develop habits that either economically enslave or empower our children. What will our words and actions reveal about our choices? By sharing this book with the young people in our lives, I truly believe that we will help them build the foundation for a successful future.

Let's prepare our children. They deserve the right to become responsible, confident adults, equipped with the knowledge that will allow them to have the greatest possible opportunity to participate in the American dream.

Sam X Renick

Sam X Renick
CEO & Founder
The **It's A Habit!** Company, Inc.

Guess the Chapter Titles

A fun and unique feature of this book is that you get to guess the chapter titles as if you were the author of the book. The total number of words in each chapter is located in parentheses below. Clues are contained in each chapter, especially on the first and last pages. If you can find the main idea of each chapter, you will probably guess the chapter titles. The answers are located on the last page of each chapter. Put on your detective hat and see if you can solve the title for each chapter. Good luck!

Contents

Chapter One
"The ___"

Hi! My name is Sammy. I know a secret.
It's a secret that I'll never forget.

It all started one summer day. I asked my sisters and big brother if I could play with them.

"No way!" they shouted back, as usual.

"Pleeeease," I begged.

"Leave us alone!" demanded my brother.

"They never want to play with me," I mumbled to my dog as we walked down the road.

I was so upset, I tripped over my drooping ears and discovered the most beautiful sight that I had ever seen. Carrots! Lots of big juicy carrots.

I rushed to pick them, gobbling them as fast as I could.
I ate only my favorite part and threw the rest away.

Minutes later, we plopped to the ground. I was so stuffed that I thought my stomach was going to explode!

Out of nowhere a voice called, "Good morning, Sammy! Will you help me collect nuts?"

"Uhhh...okay, Auntie Squirly."

Immediately, Auntie noticed all the carrots on the ground and asked, "Sammy, aren't you going to save what's left of those carrots instead of wasting them?"

"Why Auntie?" I replied. "Carrots are growing everywhere."

"Sammy, may I share a secret with you?"

"A secret! I *love* secrets. Please tell me."

"The secret," she whispered, "is that **saving is a habit**, Sammy Rabbit!"

Were you able to guess the title of **Chapter One**? "The Secret"

Chapter Two
"Saving is ____!"

"Sammy, a habit is something we do every day. I'll never forget getting lost in the woods as a child. Thank goodness I had made a **habit of saving** nuts every day. Luckily, they lasted until my mother found me, or I could have starved."

10

"It's smart to save a little every day," she said.

"You're right, Auntie! I'll start saving right away."

"Sammy, I've got a surprise for you. You can store all your savings in this backpack."

"Wow! Thanks, Auntie!"

On the way home, I stuffed my backpack with carrots and kept repeating the secret, **"Saving is a habit! Saving is a habit!"**

That night, I hid my collection of carrots in my treasure chest. I couldn't sleep, because I kept imagining how many carrots I'd have if I saved every day. Auntie's secret kept repeating in my head: **"Saving is a habit! Saving is a habit!"**

13

As soon as the sun came up, I grabbed my backpack and went out to collect more carrots. I saved a backpack full of carrots every day for weeks.

My
Pa
in
sav

"I'l

Ma
sto

After everyone was asleep and the lights were out, my dog and I would crawl under the bed and count carrots. My savings kept getting bigger and bigger. It was fun watching it grow.

Were you able to guess the title of **Chapter Two**? "Saving is a habit!"

Soon after Papa left, the wind howled and shook our house back and forth. We all screamed - even my big brother, and he's not afraid of anything.

The storm grew fiercer by the minute. We all worried
why Papa was taking so long.

"Mama, when's Papa coming home?" asked my brother
nervously.

"We're hungry," said my sisters.

"Gather around kids," said Mama. "Papa went to the storage shed. He must be caught in the storm, and there isn't any food in the house."

"Oh no!" cried my brother and sisters.

Were you able to guess the title of **Chapter Three**? "The Storm"

Chapter Four
"Sammy ___ __ __!"

Just then, the front door burst open.
"Papa! Auntie!" everyone shouted with relief.

Mama was shaking as she hugged Papa and asked about the food.

"Mama," he replied, "the storm has ruined everything. It flooded Auntie's house and destroyed our shed. It washed away all the food we were saving."

"No!" said Mama. "What will we do now?"

I grabbed Auntie's hand and said, "Come with me."

"Sammy, where are you taking me?" she asked.

"Look," I said, proudly pointing to my stash of carrots.

"Come here, everyone!" Auntie happily called to the others.

23

"Sammy!" exclaimed Mama.
"Where did you get all those carrots?"

"I've been saving them since Auntie
shared her secret with me."

22

"You saved the day," said Mama.

"Yes, Sammy, you saved the day," said Papa. "Now we'll be able to eat all winter!"

Were you able to guess the title of **Chapter Four**? *"Sammy Saves the Day!"*

Chapter Five
"The _____"

"What secret did Auntie share with you?" asked my brother and sisters.

"If I tell you, do you promise to let me play with you from now on?"

"We promise!" they all shouted together.

"**Saving is a habit**, silly rabbits!" I replied.

Early the next morning, my brother and sisters jumped onto my bed. "Wake up, Sammy! Will you come help us find and save carrots?" they asked.

"Yeah, let's go," I replied with a big smile.

As we walked and collected carrots, I thought to myself, *Hmmm...what should I promise to save for next?*

Were you able to guess the title of **Chapter 5**? "The Promise"

New Words Mean More Mental Muscle Power!

Once we learn new words, they are ours to save and use forever. Most of the words in this story are at a second grade level or lower, so you are probably already familiar with them. But listed below there are some harder words at higher reading levels. See if you can find them in the story.

Key Word List!

1. **Saving** - Saving means putting something away to use at another time. Saving also means that we do not spend everything we have right now.
2. **Habit** - A habit is something that we do over and over again. Habits can be good or bad. Saving is an example of a good habit. If we always put away part of the money we receive, we are making saving a habit.
3. **Mission** - A specific goal that a person or group of persons is attempting to perform.
4. **Execute** - To perform or carry out your plans or goals.

Game!

Can you find these words in the story?

1. **Burst** – to suddenly break open. Page _____
2. **Collect** – to gather together. Page _____
3. **Exclaimed** – to speak out loudly with strong feeling. Page _____
4. **Explode** – to grow very big, very fast. Page _____
5. **Immediately** – right away. Page _____
6. **Fiercer** – even more fierce; dangerously wild. Page _____
7. **Grabbed** – to suddenly take hold of. Page _____
8. **Howled** – to make a long, loud cry or noise, like the wind or a dog can make.
   Page _____
9. **Repeating** – saying or doing again. Page _____
10. **Streaked** – a long, skinny mark that goes by very quickly, like lightning when it rains. Page _____
11. **Drooping** – to sink, bend, sag, or hang down. Page _____
12. **Demanded** – to ask for right away with force. Page _____

Note: Remember, words can have more than one meaning or definition. We've included the definition of the word as it is used in the story.

Executing the Mission - Helping Kids to Save!

Sam X Renick
The Author

Sam X Renick (a.k.a. Sam, Sam the Money Man) is CEO and Founder of The **It's A Habit!** Company, Inc. and primary author of 'It's A Habit, Sammy Rabbit!' He is a native of Los Angeles, a graduate of Loyola Marymount University, and a practicing financial and insurance consultant.

Juan Alvarado
The Illustrator

Juan Alvarado is lead illustrator and a shareholder in The **It's A Habit!** Company. Juan is self-taught and has been practicing his craft on a daily basis since age six.

What other readers have to say!

"I really enjoyed reading 'It's A Habit, Sammy Rabbit!' I particularly enjoyed guessing the chapter titles. That was fun! It's also unique. The message – saving is a habit – is an important one for today's youth and comes across very clearly to the reader. This is a book every child and parent should read."
Dr. Katy Merrill, *1999-2000 California Principal of the Year*

"The earlier we get kids to understand the value of smart money skills, like saving, the better. Books like 'It's A Habit, Sammy Rabbit!' [are] key tools in the quest to arm every child in America with the financial smarts [needed] to succeed in the real world."
United States Congressman David Dreier

"I want to save money like the rabbit."
Juan, *Grade 2*

"I think the whole family should read the story together and learn about saving money...."
Audrey, *Grade 3*

"I started to save the next day...and I told my friend Brenda and she started saving, and I told my mom and she started saving."
Juliana, *Grade 4*

The **It's A Habit!** Company, Inc.
The **It's A Habit!** Company, Inc. is a multilingual publishing and promotional company dedicated to sharing the "saving is a habit" message with children of all ages through fun and entertaining products and services. The **It's A Habit!** Company, Inc. mission:
Changing Children's Lives One Dime at a Time!